MARC BROWN

ARTHUR'S CLASSROOM FIB

Random House 🏠 New York

STEP INTO READING, RANDOM HOUSE, and the Random House colophon are registered trademarks of Random House, Inc. ARTHUR is a registered trademark of Marc Brown.

www.stepintoreading.com

Educators and librarians, for a variety of teaching tools, visit us at www.randomhouse.com/teachers

Library of Congress Cataloging-in-Publication Data
Brown, Marc Tolon.
Arthur's classroom fib / Marc Brown. — 1st ed.
p. cm.
SUMMARY: After hearing about the exciting summer vacations of his classmates, Arthur decides to write an embellished version of his own summer experiences.
ISBN 978-0-375-82975-8 (trade) — ISBN 978-0-375-92975-5 (lib. bdg.)
[1. Aardvark—Fiction. 2. Animals—Fiction. 3. Honesty—Fiction. 4. Vacations—Fiction.
5. Schools—Fiction. 6. Brothers and sisters—Fiction.] I. Title.
PZ7.B81618Aokc 2007 [E]—dc22 2005037110

Printed in the United States of America 10 9 8 7 6 5 4 3 2 1 First Edition

Today was the first day
of school.

"Listen up, boys and girls,"
said Mr. Ratburn.

"Here is your homework
for tomorrow."
Everyone groaned.
"Write about your summer."

After school Arthur's friends
talked about their summers.

Muffy went around the world
on a ship.

Binky went to Disney World.

Francine went to tennis camp.

She won a gold cup.

The Brain went to computer camp.

He built his own computer.

Buster flew in his dad's plane
all around America.
"Maybe I'll write about
my visit to the White House.
Or maybe about the alligator farm
in Florida," he said.

"What are you going to write about?" he asked Arthur.

"I'm thinking," said Arthur.

After dinner Arthur tried
to write his report.
"Everyone went somewhere,
but we went nowhere,"
said Arthur to D.W.
"We went to the beach
on Sundays," she said.

8

"Going to the beach on Sundays
is not exciting," he said.
Then Arthur had an idea.
"I'll play with you later,
but I need to write now."
"Okay," said D.W., and she left.
This is what Arthur wrote:

"I had the most exciting summer.
One day at the beach,
a big wave swept
my little sister D.W. out to sea.
I jumped on my surfboard
to save her."

"But just as I reached D.W.,

an octopus pulled her under.

I dove in.

I punched the octopus.

It let go of D.W.

But now a shark

was swimming toward us!"

"We got on my surfboard
and rode a big wave
back to the beach
before the shark could get us.
I was a hero."

Arthur read his report out loud.

"This is great!" he said.

D.W. marched into his room.

"It's a great big fib!"
she shouted.

"And you'll be
in big trouble with it."

The next day at school,
Arthur gave his report.
"I had the most exciting summer,"
he began.

Then he stopped reading
and put down his paper.
"We stayed home all summer,"
he said.
"What's exciting about that?"
whispered Binky to Buster.

"We stayed home,"
Arthur continued,
"because we got
a brand-new baby!
And I named her Baby Kate.

This is what she looks like."
Arthur showed the photos
of Baby Kate.
"Oh, she's so cute," said Francine.
"I wish I had a baby sister,"
said Binky.

"I can make her smile,"
said Arthur.
"I make funny faces.
And I can make her stop crying.
I rock her back and forth
and sing to her."

Arthur told the class
all about Baby Kate.
"And she looks just like me,"
he said as he finished his report.
Everyone clapped and cheered.

"Good report, Arthur,"
said Mr. Ratburn.
"It came from your heart.
Getting a new baby sister
IS exciting.
We all enjoyed hearing
about your new baby sister."

At home Arthur told D.W.

all about his report.

D.W. stamped her foot.

"You told a big fib, Arthur.

Baby Kate does not

look like you,"

she said.

"Baby Kate looks like me!"